For all bright-eyed, bright owl readers.

Library of Congress Cataloging-in-Publication Data
Names: Coxe, Molly, author, illustrator.
Title: Cubs in a tub / by Molly Coxe.
Description: First Kane Press Edition. | New York : Kane Press, [2018] |
"Originally published in different form by BraveMouse Books in 2015"—Title page
verso. | Summary: One snowy day, bear cubs Russ and Gus are bored with staying
inside until they use their imaginations to make a sled from a wash tub.
Identifiers: LCCN 2018007761 (print) | LCCN 2017038646 (ebook) | ISBN 9781575659862
(ebook) | ISBN 9781575659855 (pbk) | ISBN 9781575659848 (reinforced library binding)
Subjects: | CYAC: Bears—Fiction. | Animals—Infancy—Fiction. | Imagination—Fiction. | Sleds—
Fiction.
Classification: LCC PZ7.C839424 (print) | LCC PZ7.C839424 Cu 2018 (ebook) |
DDC [E]—dc23
LC record available at https://lccn.loc.gov/2018007761

10 9 8 7 6 5 4 3 2 1

Printed in China

Book Design: Michelle Martinez

Bright Owl Books is a
trademark of Kane Press, Inc.

Visit us online at
www.kanepress.com

 Follow us on Twitter
@KanePress

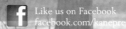 Like us on Facebook
facebook.com/kanepress

Cubs in a TUB

by Molly Coxe

Kane Press • New York

Russ and Gus
are stuck in the hut
with Mum and Hunny.
"Ho hum," says Gus.
"Ho hum," says Russ.

"Don't be glum," says Mum.
"Let's have some fun!"
says Gus.

Two cubs. One tub.
Russ mutters.
Gus putters.

"Tug!" says Gus.
"I am tugging!" says Russ.

"Run!" says Russ.
"I am running!" says Gus.

"Cowabunga!"

Russ and Gus rush
past Muff and Fluff.

"Hi, Muff," says Russ.
"Hi, Fluff," says Gus.

Uh-oh!

Jumps!

Bumps!

Lumps!

"My tum!" says Russ.
"My bum!" says Gus.

"Is that Mum and Hunny?"
asks Russ.

"Mum!"

Mum tugs the tub
up, up, up.

"One more run?" asks Mum.
"Look!" says Russ.
"Hunny wants to come!"

"Cowabunga!"

Story Starters

Mum is humming.
What is she humming?

Muff and Fluff are stuck in the mud.
What will Muff and Fluff do?